PUFFIN B(

GW01081487

Lucky's C

Betsy Duffey was born in ~~Sout~~
United States of America. She is the daughter of
the acclaimed children's writer, Betsy Byars. Betsy
Duffey has written a number of books for children,
and currently lives in Atlanta, Georgia, with her
husband and two sons.

Some other books by Betsy Duffey

LUCKY ON THE LOOSE
A BOY IN THE DOGHOUSE

For older readers

BUSTER AND THE BLACK HOLE
HOW TO BE COOL IN JUNIOR SCHOOL

Betsy Duffey

Lucky's Christmas

Illustrated by Shelagh McNicholas

PUFFIN BOOKS

PUFFIN BOOKS

Published by the Penguin Group
Penguin Books Ltd, 27 Wrights Lane, London W8 5TZ, England
Penguin Books USA Inc., 375 Hudson Street, New York, New York 10014, USA
Penguin Books Australia Ltd, Ringwood, Victoria, Australia
Penguin Books Canada Ltd, 10 Alcorn Avenue, Toronto, Ontario, Canada M4V 3B2
Penguin Books (NZ) Ltd, Private Bag 102902, NSMC, Auckland 10, New Zealand

Penguin Books Ltd, Registered Offices: Harmondsworth, Middlesex, England

First published in the United States by Simon & Schuster Books for Young Readers,
a Divison of Simon and Schuster, Inc. 1994
First published in Great Britain by Viking 1995
Published in Puffin Books 1997
3 5 7 9 10 8 6 4

Filmset in Garamond

Made and printed in England by Clays Ltd, St Ives plc

British Library Cataloguing in Publication Data
A CIP catalogue record for this book is available from the British Library
ISBN 0–140–37599–6

Contents

Aunt Octopus

George was packing his things into a cardboard box. His baseball glove. His bat. His collection of baseball cards.

His mother's aunt, Aunt Octavia, was coming for Christmas. And she was staying in HIS room.

There were some good things about Aunt Octavia. He liked the way she looked – soft and wrinkled. He liked the way she smelled – like cinnamon. She always had time to play cards with him and she told wonderful stories. But there were other things about her that he did not like.

She always wrapped her arms around

him and *squeezed* like an octopus. Aunt Octopus, George called her.

She would say, 'How's my favourite nephew? Now give us a hug!'

She would smother him with octopus hugs. Then she would slime him with octopus kisses.

It was too horrible to think about.

George packed his special model car and his space rock. He looked at the rest of the stuff on his shelf and sighed. The box was too small for everything.

He hoped Aunt Octopus wouldn't touch his things. 'Tidy up,' she called it. When she 'tidied up,' it meant getting rid of his stuff. Good stuff, too.

Once she threw out his insect collection. It had taken him weeks to gather all the insects. 'Unhygienic,' she said. Then in one flush they were gone.

He hoped Aunt Octavia wouldn't offer to cook. She always made casseroles. Mixtures of things with strange names. Gazpacho or Boeuf Bourguignon. Once he saw a fish eye in one. His mother said it was a black olive but he was never sure about it.

He hoped that she hadn't bought his Christmas present at a car boot sale this year. Last year she had given him a glow-in-the-dark painting of Elvis Presley on black velvet. Elvis stared at him from above the bed. His mother always put it up when Aunt Octopus came.

His aunt loved that painting. She always walked into his room and talked to it. She'd say, 'Elvis, you hound dog!'

Most of all, he hoped that she would like Lucky. On her last visit George had not had a dog. Lucky stared at him from the bottom of the bed.

Lucky's brown eyes watched George as he packed. George put Lucky's rubber newspaper in the box. Lucky whined.

Aunt Octopus didn't seem like the kind of person who would like dogs. George remembered the insect collection. It didn't look good for Lucky. 'You're not un-hygienic, are you?' he asked Lucky. Lucky thumped his tail.

George picked up the box and walked to his parents' bedroom. His sleeping bag was already rolled out on the floor.

'I'll be sleeping here,' he told Lucky.

Lucky jumped on to the sleeping bag. He rolled over and rubbed his back.

'Remember, Lucky, don't jump up on Aunt Octopus.'

Erf!

'And don't chew any of her things.'

Erf!

'And don't bark at her.'

Erf! Erf!

George reached over and picked up Lucky.

George buried his face in Lucky's back. 'It's only for two days,' he said. 'Just be good for two days. Just until Christmas is over.'

'George, is your room ready?' George's

mother hurried in, carrying an armload of towels.

'Yes.'

'Remember, George, be polite to your aunt.'

'OK.'

'And leave her bedroom alone.'

'OK!'

'And have nice manners at the table.'

'OK! OK!'

Honk! Honk!

George and his mother looked out the window. A big black car was pulling into the driveway. George could see grey hair and two octopus arms holding the steering wheel – Aunt Octopus.

Honk! Honk!

'Let's go down,' George's mother said. 'And, George, *please*, remember your manners.'

George's mother hurried out of the bedroom and down the stairs.

'Come on, Lucky.' George put Lucky down. 'She's here.'

Honk! Honk!

'Let's go down. And, Lucky, *please*, remember your manners.'

Dog Greetings

Honk! Honk!

Lucky raced down the stairs. To Lucky, the sound of a horn meant visitors, and Lucky loved visitors. When people came to visit they always patted him and rubbed him behind the ears. One of his most important jobs was to welcome new people.

Lucky had lived with the boy for almost a year now. He knew what his jobs were.

When the boy threw the rubber newspaper, Lucky was expected to chase it and bring it back to the boy. When he did this the boy said, 'Good dog!'

Lucky was expected to clean up any bits of food dropped on the floor when his family was eating. When he did this the woman said, 'Good dog!'

He was expected to protect his family. He barked when someone came to the door or when strangers came into the back garden. He kept the squirrels from coming on to the back porch. When he did this the man said, 'Good dog!'

He also had learned some things that he was *not* to do.

Roll on dead things.

Make puddles in the house.

Chew George's baseball glove.

When he did these things his people said, 'Bad dog!' The rules were clear. The rules made him feel safe.

He ran out of the house into the driveway. A visitor was getting out of a car. Lucky was just in time. Everyone was hugging her.

Lucky bounded down the driveway at

full speed. He got ready for his typical greeting – sniffs and licks and pats. He neared the people. He stopped short.

Sniff. Sniff.

There was a new scent in the air.

Sniff. Sniff.

The smell was coming from the front seat of the visitor's car.

It was an animal smell. The car door was open. Lucky hurried over for a better look.

Yes, his nose had not failed him. There on the front seat of the car was an animal.

It did not look like the squirrels Lucky chased up the oak tree. It did not look like the tabby cat next door.

It was a different kind of animal. It was white with curly hair.

Lucky knew what to do when he met a new animal. It was his job to protect his people. He had to show right away who was boss.

He raised the hair on his back and let out a low growl.

GGRRRRR!

The car animal did not answer.

GGRRRRR! He growled again.

Still no answer.

Lucky's visitor manners were forgotten. He had to protect his people. He guessed the distance. He jumped.

He soared right into the car. Direct hit. He attacked the animal.

He sunk his teeth into the animal's skin and shook his head back and forth. What was it? It was an animal but not an animal. It was something wild and furry.

He dragged it out on to the driveway for a better fight. He must protect his people.

The woman screamed. 'Auntie's coat!' she said. 'Auntie's sheepskin coat!'

GGRRRR!

Lucky shook his head again.

The man grabbed Lucky by the back of the neck and pulled. Lucky would not let himself be pulled away. He sank his teeth deeper into the soft car animal.

'Help!'

The man pulled harder but Lucky would not let go.

The scent of animal was all around him now.

He had smelled some wonderful things in his life. Ham, cheese, a frog squashed on the road.

But this was different. This was new. This was the most wonderful, wild, irresistible smell he had ever experienced.

He shook his jaws back and forth.

GRRR!

AAAAAAAAAA!

Down came a bag on Lucky's head. The man pulled harder. Lucky's jaws came loose.

Lucky didn't feel the pain. He didn't feel the roughness of the man jerking him away. His attention was fixed on the animal. It lay in the driveway, not moving.

He had shown it who was boss. He had done his job.

Lucky wagged his tail and looked up at the man. He waited to hear the words: 'Good dog.'

But the man looked down at Lucky and pointed his finger and said the other words: 'Bad dog!'

Slimed!

'Lucky!' George yelled. He ran over to Lucky. He patted him to calm him down. It didn't work. George's father held Lucky tightly in his arms.

Lucky fought to get free. He made swimming motions with his feet in the air in the direction of the sheepskin jacket. His eyes rolled with the effort. He barked and squirmed.

'Bad dog!' George's father said again.

'It's OK!' Aunt Octopus said. 'It's just an old jacket. I got it at a car boot sale.'

'It is *not* OK,' said George's mother, looking at Lucky. 'That dog should know better.'

'It really *is* OK.'

'Let's go inside.'

George's mother led Aunt Octopus towards the house. George watched them walk away. Aunt Octopus had a red track-suit on. A picture of Father Christmas was painted on the front. Her grey hair was pulled back in a bun. It was strange to see clothes like that on someone so old.

Aunt Octopus turned and winked at George. He didn't say a word. When his mother called Lucky 'that dog' it was time to be quiet.

He turned back to Lucky. Lucky had stopped wriggling. He patted Lucky. Lucky wagged his tail and licked George's hand.

George smiled.

Lucky had saved him! No Octopus hugs this time! In all the excitement Aunt Octopus had forgotten. For once he wouldn't be slimed. No kisses and hugs for him!

But . . . He watched Aunt Octopus

walk towards the house. It was not a good beginning. She patted the sheepskin jacket as she walked up the stairs to the porch.

Erf!

When she touched the jacket Lucky lunged forward again.

George had never seen Lucky get so excited.

George's mother frowned back at George. They disappeared into the house.

'What's got into Lucky?' said George's father.

George shook his head. 'I don't know. Maybe he thinks that jacket is an animal.'

'Lucky had better behave himself while your aunt is here.'

George nodded. 'He'll be good. He was just excited about having visitors.'

George's father looked at Lucky. 'We'll see how it goes,' he said. 'But for today let's keep him outside.'

'It's Christmas Eve, Dad. Lucky needs to be with us.'

'I'm sorry, son. We can't have Lucky behaving badly with a visitor here.'

George took Lucky from his father and held him close.

'You know we all have to be on our best behaviour this week,' said George's father.

He looked at Lucky. 'And that means Lucky too.'

'Be good, Lucky,' George said, 'or else.'

'Just a minute,' Aunt Octopus called from the porch. She hurried down the steps. The jacket was gone.

Lucky's fur stood up. In one leap he was on the ground. His nose sniffed the air.

She headed towards George, her arms stretched out wide.

'I didn't even say a proper hello to George. How's my favourite nephew? Now give us a hug!'

Before George could move, it happened.

Octopus arms!

'And a big, *big* kiss for my favourite nephew.'

SMACK!

George wiped his face with the back of his hand.

Slimed!

The Broken Record Bark

She had gone. *It* had gone. The car animal was inside the house.

Lucky ran up the steps and pressed his nose against the crack at the back door and sniffed. He could not even get a whiff of the animal.

'Move, Lucky.'

With his foot the boy pushed Lucky off the step. The boy walked up the steps and went into the house. The man walked up the steps and went into the house.

Lucky walked up the steps and . . .

BAM!

The door slammed shut. He was left outside.

He waited. George would let him in. He scratched the door a few times. George did not come.

Being left outside had to do with the words *Bad dog*.

He hated those words. They always meant that something bad was about to happen to him. Like a whack on the behind or being put outside. They meant that a rule had been broken.

Lucky sniffed at the door again. He thought he had obeyed all the rules. He had not bitten or drooled on anyone. He had not allowed the car animal to harm his family. He had greeted the visitor. No! He had *not* greeted the visitor! That must be it. He must greet the visitor.

First, though, he had to work out how to get into the house.

A bark might work.

Lucky tried to remember his barking lessons. His mother had taught him many different kinds of bark. There was the Chain Letter Bark.

He used that bark at night. When the dog down the street barked, then Lucky would bark back. Then the dog *across* the street would bark and so on. That would not work now.

There was the Demand Bark. One short bark to show his people what he wanted.

Erf!

He barked at the back door. Now they would open it and let him in.

Erf!

Nobody came. Maybe they hadn't heard him.

He tried it again.

Erf!

Still nothing.

Maybe this situation called for a different bark. The Broken Record Bark. You bark over and over like a broken record.

Erf! Erf! Erf! Erf! Erf! Erf! Erf!

It tortures your people into giving you what you want. He had used it once to teach the boy that he didn't like his

doghouse. He would use it now to get the boy to let him into the house.

Erf! Erf! Erf! Erf! Erf! Erf! Erf!

No George.

Erf! Erf! Erf! Erf! Erf! Erf! Erf!

The door swung open.

'Bad dog!' said the man.

The door swung shut.

Lucky rested his head on his front paws. Those words again. He rolled his eyes up at the door and watched and waited.

Bad dog. The words echoed in his mind. He had heard those terrible words twice today. It was not a good day for Lucky.

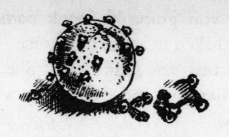

Memories

George sat with his parents and his aunt in the living room. Christmas Eve was usually the best day of the year.

The house smelled right. The turkey cooking in the oven. The baubles for the tree. The pine branches on the mantelpiece.

Everything looked right. Christmas candles twinkled. The ornaments waited in a red box for the tree.

But it didn't feel right. It was hard to enjoy Christmas Eve with Lucky outside.

Aunt Octopus straightened in her chair. She picked up a brown carrier bag from beside her feet.

'Are you going to cook something?' George asked in a worried voice.

'Not this year,' she said. She opened the carrier bag and pulled out a sack of oranges.

'Come here, George,' she said. 'I'll show you how we used to make pomanders.'

'What's a pomander?'

'Come and see.'

He moved over and sat on the floor beside his aunt. She pulled out a small jar of cloves and began to push them into an orange.

George took a clove and an orange and tried it.

'This smells good,' he said.

'This is what I used to give my mother and my sister, Mary, for Christmas every year. They kept them in bowls around the house to make the rooms smell good.'

'An old-fashioned air freshener,' said George.

Everyone laughed. 'I remember them in Grandma's house,' said George's mother.

'I just love coming here for Christmas,' said Aunt Octopus. 'It reminds me of Christmases long ago.'

'Tell us what it was like,' said George's father.

George scooted closer to Aunt Octavia. If he couldn't be with Lucky, at least he could hear a story. He pushed a few more cloves into his orange and listened.

'One year Mary gave me a hat for Christmas. I still remember it. A blue pillbox hat with a tiny veil and a feather on the side.'

It sounded silly to George. He looked at the door.

'We both loved that hat. The next year I gave the hat back to her for Christmas. I can still see her face when she opened that box.'

'Was she cross?' George couldn't imagine giving anyone a used present.

'No,' said Aunt Octopus. 'She was glad.'

'She liked it?'

'She loved it.'

'But it was old.'

'It didn't matter to her. She loved it anyway.'

George wasn't thinking about Lucky now. He smiled.

'So the next year, guess what she gave me.'

'The hat?'

'The hat.'

George laughed. 'Recycled!' he said.

'We gave each other that same hat for twenty years. Until she died.'

Aunt Octopus dabbed her eyes. 'I never laughed so hard as I did every Christmas morning when I saw that silly hat.'

'Did you have a Christmas tree?' George asked.

'Of course,' she said. 'And we had a special tree for the whole town. We had it in the church and everyone would come and bring decorations for it. It would be covered with candles and the ornaments would be gifts.'

'What kind of gifts?'

'Small things. A pomander.' She held up her orange and smiled. 'A handkerchief for a man or a piece of fruit for a child. If you liked a certain girl or fellow you would put a gift on the tree for him.'

'Did you ever do that?'

She nodded and smiled. 'The crossest I ever got with Mary was over a gift on that Christmas tree.'

'The hat?'

'Not the hat. It's another story. I'll tell you sometime.'

She put down her orange. It was covered with cloves now.

'Talking about gifts reminds me,' she said. 'I am making a special surprise for *you* for Christmas and I'm going upstairs right now to finish it.'

'You don't need to tidy up or anything, do you?' George held his breath.

'No, your room is perfect.'

She walked up the stairs. As she walked into George's bedroom they could hear her say, 'Elvis, you hound dog!'

Everyone smiled.

George's father stood up.

'Come on, George,' he said. 'We've got a job to do too. It's time to bring in our Christmas tree.'

George jumped up and hurried to the back door with his father. He loved decorating the tree.

They had chosen it the night before at the Boy Scout tree sale.

It was tall and even with a single point on the top. The perfect tree. It was out in the garage.

Lucky barked and wagged his tail when he saw them.

'Can Lucky help?' George asked. 'Aunt Octavia is in her room. He can't bother her.'

'OK,' said George's father. 'We'll give

him another chance. But he has to be on his best behaviour.'

'He will be,' said George. 'He will.'

Oh, Christmas Tree

When Lucky had almost given up hope, the door swung open. Out walked the man and the boy.

Lucky jumped up. He wriggled and wagged his tail. The boy picked him up and petted him all over.

He was forgiven. Now he would be good. He would follow the rules.

'Come on, Lucky,' George called.

George and the man walked towards the garage. Lucky followed them. The man pulled up the garage door.

Lucky hurried along beside George. If they were going for a ride he did not want to be left behind.

He ran into the garage. He stopped. He sniffed. A tree was standing in the corner!

Lucky poked his nose into the air. He sniffed the tree. It was a fresh tree with the smells of the forest still on it.

He moved closer.

What was a tree doing inside the garage?

The man picked up one end of the tree. George picked up the other. They began to carry it towards the house.

The tree was going inside the house!

Lucky wagged his tail and sniffed the tree again as it went up the stairs. He danced back and forth behind the tree. That was exciting!

They carried the tree into the living room and stopped. Lucky cocked his head and watched.

The man put the tree down. He hammered something on to the bottom of the tree and stood it up. Lucky's family stood back and looked at the tree.

Lucky looked at his family, then back at the tree.

Lucky knew what trees were for!

When he was a puppy he made puddles like this: he would sniff, circle three times, squat and make a puddle

When he grew up he made puddles a different way: he would find a tree, sniff it, circle it three times, then lift his back leg.

Now as he looked at the tree he was confused. Puddles were not allowed in the house. A tree had been brought into the house. Trees were for puddles. Had the rules changed?

Were puddles now allowed in the house? Was this his own personal indoor tree?

Dog Heaven!

He looked at the tree one more time.

Should he or shouldn't he?

Lucky moved closer to the tree.

He sniffed it.

No one said *Bad dog*.

He circled it three times.
Still no *Bad dog*.
He lifted his back leg.
'Bad dog!'

Silent Night, Howly Night

ERF! ERF!

George lay in his sleeping bag on the floor of his parents' bedroom. His parents were asleep. He was not. Lucky was barking. Outside. In the doghouse.

It had been the worst Christmas Eve ever. Lucky had been in trouble three times.

He had attacked Aunt Octopus's jacket. Then he had barked at the door. Then the Christmas tree incident.

Now he was banned from the house until Aunt Octopus went home. It wasn't Lucky's fault. Everything changed when visitors came. It was Aunt Octopus's fault.

44

ERF! ERF!

George squeezed his eyes shut. He couldn't fall asleep. Lucky was alone out in the doghouse.

Lucky was probably cold. Worst of all, he would wake up George's mother and father and Aunt Octopus.

AAOOOOOOOOO!

He had to do something. He remembered when Lucky was a puppy. Lucky would bark like this in the back garden until George went out and slept with him.

That was in the summer. Now it was too cold for George to sleep in the doghouse. He hoped it wasn't too cold for Lucky.

ERF! ERF!

Christmas should be a happy time. He was not happy.

He tried to think about something else. He thought about his stocking hanging up by the fireplace. He hoped he would get a bike for Christmas. A mountain bike. He had given his mother three pomanders and a sign he had painted. It said, GOOD FOR FREE HUGS ANY TIME. He smiled. She would love it.

Erf! Erf!

The gift for his father was a pottery dinosaur he had made at school. Blue glaze. He smiled. His dad would love it.

Erf! Erf!

He didn't have anything for his aunt. His mother had said they would give her one present from the whole family. It was a certificate for ten dance lessons at a dance studio. She would love it. She wanted to learn the mambo.

Erf! Erf!

And Lucky – Lucky was getting a new chew bone, a rubber squeaky toy, and some treats.

George pulled the pillow over his head. He began to hum a Christmas carol.

'Joy to the world . . .' He stopped. He was not joyful.

He tried another one.

'Si-lent night' – *AAOOOOOOO!*

'Ho-ly night' – *AAOOOOOOOOO!*

'All is calm' – *AOOOOOO!*

'All is bright' – *AAOOOOOOO!*

George couldn't stand it any more. He crawled out of the sleeping bag and tip-toed out of the room.

As he tiptoed past his bedroom, he heard a snore. Aunt Octopus was asleep in his bed.

He ran downstairs and outside.

The frosty grass stung his feet through his socks. He ran over to Lucky and reached down to undo the chain.

Lucky was shivering.

George picked him up and held him close. Lucky licked George's face. George carried Lucky back to the house.

He put Lucky down. Lucky ran straight to the fridge. He curled up in a ball in front of the vent where the warm air blew.

Lucky was not shivering now. Surely it would be OK to leave him here.

'I trust you, Lucky,' George whispered. 'I know that you won't do anything else bad.'

Lucky didn't move or wag his tail. His eyes were closed. He was fast asleep.

George turned and tiptoed back upstairs. Back past Aunt Octopus snoring in his bed. Back to his sleeping bag on the floor of his parents' room.

He heard the steady sounds of their breathing. They had not heard George leave or come back.

In the morning they might be angry because he had let Lucky in. But this would be a way for him to show them that Lucky could behave.

He closed his eyes. He thought once more about Lucky sleeping in front of the fridge. He hoped he was right.

Wake-up Duty

Lucky stretched and opened his eyes. Morning was his favourite time of day.

He loved waking up in front of the fridge. He loved the warm air that blew out of the vent and warmed the spot on the floor where he slept.

He loved the feeling of a good stretch. One leg first and then the other.

But most of all he loved wake-up duty. It was his job to wake up the boy.

The woman would usually say: 'Go get George.'

And he would run upstairs, jump on the boy's bed, dig in the covers and lick the boy until his eyes opened. Then they would wrestle on the bed. The boy would laugh and hug him and they would go downstairs for breakfast.

Licks and hugs. Pats and wrestles. Lucky loved wake-up duty.

He got up and stretched, one leg first and then the other. The boy's mother was not awake yet. But it was time.

He ran upstairs into the boy's room. He ran in and stopped.

There was a suitcase on the floor. It was open. He hurried over to get a better look.

Sniff. Sniff. What was inside?

Some clothes.

Sniff. Sniff.

He smelled the clothes. These were the clothes of the visitor. The visitor who had brought the car animal. Maybe the animal was in here!

Wake-up duty was forgotten.

He began to dig in the clothes. He used his best digging motion.

Paw over paw.

Clothes flew in all directions.

Paw over paw.

He had to get to the bottom. He nosed in deeper and deeper . . .

No animal.

He lifted his head and looked around the room.

He saw the bed. George. He had almost forgotten wake-up duty!

He stretched once more for good measure. Then headed for the bed.

With one quick jump he was on the bed.

Erf!

He dug into the mound of covers. Time for hugs and pats. Licks and wrestles.

Erf!

Paw over paw he dug into George's bed.

George would wake up and hug him and pat him and . . .

'AAAEEEEEEE!'

It was not George!

Lucky struggled to get away.

'AEEEEEE!' the visitor screamed.

Lucky was a brave dog. He was not afraid of the tabby cat next door, or the garden squirrels, or even Oreo, the doberman up the street.

Up until this moment there had been only one thing in the world that Lucky was afraid of – thunder.

Any time day or night, when he heard the rumble of a thunderstorm coming his way, he knew what to do.

He would crawl under the sofa. Only there, in the darkness under the sofa, was he safe.

Now he had something new to fear. This visitor. This screaming person. This person who had taken over HIS house, HIS boy's bed.

He twisted in the covers. He could not get off the bed.

'AAEEEEE!'

The boy ran into the room.

'Lucky!' he yelled.

The rest of the family ran in.

'Lucky!' they all yelled.

Lucky twisted free. He didn't stop to hear the words *Bad dog*. He ran.

Out the door he went, down the hall, down the steps, past the indoor tree and to the only spot of true safety that he knew in the house – under the sofa.

Mrs Minnie's Kennel

George raced after his father. Down the stairs to Lucky. 'What are you going to do?' he asked.

His father didn't answer.

Zip zip zip.

His father's slippers padded down the stairs. George stayed close behind him.

'What are you going to do to Lucky?'

Still no answer.

Zip zip zip.

They walked into the living room. The tree glowed with sparkling ornaments. The stockings bulged. Brightly coloured presents waited in piles. George hurried past them. He could only think about

Lucky. George knew where he was hiding. Lucky always hid under the sofa.

George's father stopped and looked once at the sofa. Then he walked over to the telephone. He looked at a number on the book beside the phone. He started punching buttons.

'Who are you calling?' George had a bad feeling about the phone.

'Mrs Minnie.'

'The kennel?'

'Yes. Mrs Minnie's Kennel.'

'Please, Dad! Don't do it!'

He didn't stop dialling.

'George, we have to do it. We can't have Lucky and your aunt in the same house. Lucky will have to go away until after Christmas.'

He punched the last few numbers and listened.

George blinked back his tears.

George thought about Lucky being all alone. He thought about Lucky being alone for Christmas.

Lucky's presents were all wrapped under the tree. His new chew bone, his squeaky doggy toy, his treats. He would not be here to open them.

Lucky's stocking was hanging by the fireplace next to George's. He would not be here to see what Santa brought him.

He thought about how much Lucky would love Christmas carols. He would point his nose into the air and sing with them. *Aaaoooooo!* He would not be singing any carols at Mrs Minnie's Kennel.

He had to be home for Christmas.

'You can't, Dad!'

'I can.'

George could not hold the tears back now.

'Please, Dad. One more chance.'

His father shook his head.

'Why can't Aunt Octopus go home instead?' George said. 'She's the one causing the problem, not Lucky!'

George was shouting now. 'Lucky behaved himself properly before she came!'

'Now, George. Calm down.'

'I hate her! She's just an old octopus and I hate her!'

'George!'

George looked at his father.

He hung up the phone. He was looking past George. He had a funny look on his face. George turned and followed his gaze.

Aunt Octopus was in the doorway. George's mother was next to her.

Aunt Octopus looked like someone had just knocked the wind out of her.

Her mouth was in a big O. Her eyes had a hurt look.

George's mother stared at George with her most disappointed look.

Nobody said a word.

George wished he could crawl under the sofa with Lucky.

Under the Sofa

Lucky huddled in the darkness under the sofa. He crouched low at the back in the middle. In the middle was a spot where no hands could possibly reach him.

He had learned this position when he was a puppy. He had chewed the man's briefcase. He had only chewed a little on the corner. But the man had been upset.

Lucky crouched lower and listened.

The man and the boy were talking in loud voices.

Maybe he would hear some words that he knew. Some words that would explain this terrible time.

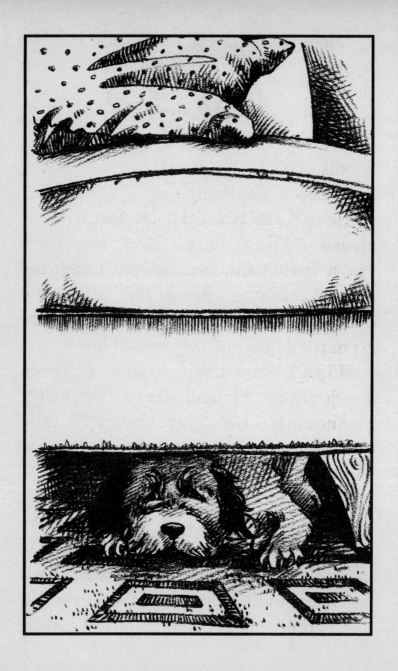

Lucky knew a lot of words. He had learned the people's language as a puppy.

He had learned the good words first — *dinner, car, walk, treat, ham,* and the best words, *GOOD DOG.* He hadn't heard any good words lately.

He had also learned some bad words — *vacuum, doghouse, vet, flea spray, kennel,* and the worst words, *Bad dog.* He had heard those words too many times.

When he had tried to defend his family from the car animal.

When he had tried to get them to open the door and let him in.

And then there was the tree problem.

Lucky closed his eyes and tried not to think about it.

There was another word, *Christmas.* He had heard that word a lot lately. He wondered what it meant. It had something to do with all the strange things that were happening.

So far *Christmas* had only meant getting

into trouble. Lucky decided that *Christmas* must be a bad word.

His heart beat faster. He kept his eyes closed.

What had happened? The morning had started out like any other morning. He had gone to wake up the boy and . . . he closed his eyes. He didn't want to think about it.

The last two days had been too confusing.

The boy was not in his room any more.

Lucky could not do anything right. It was worse than when he was a puppy.

He listened to the boy and the man. He heard some other words that he knew. Bad words, the worst words. He crouched even lower. He made himself into a tight ball.

The words were *Mrs Minnie's Kennel*.

More Memories

George sat on his parents' bed and stared at the wall. Christmas was ruined. He had ruined it.

He kept thinking about the way Aunt Octavia's face had looked when he had said that he hated her.

He didn't hate her exactly. He liked her. He had just been cross with her. Now he had ruined everything.

George brushed away a tear.

There was a knock on the door. He didn't answer. Aunt Octavia walked in.

George's throat was tight. He couldn't say anything.

'I never finished my story,' she said. 'About my sister.'

George couldn't look at her face.

'The crossest that I ever got with her was over the Christmas tree gifts.'

She sat down on the bed next to him.

'Well, there was a certain lad that we both liked. John Dadismon. He was a fine, handsome young man. The vicar's son.'

George peeped up at her.

'I embroidered a handkerchief for him one Christmas. You should have seen it. Flowers and vines and his initials on the corner. I wrapped it up and wrote on the outside: "To John, From Octavia." I hung it on the tree at church.'

She stopped for a second.

'Well, when I went outside to see if John was coming, my sister took that present from the tree. And where it said "From Octavia" she changed it to say "From Mary".'

She laughed.

'John opened that present and walked

up to Mary and kissed her on the hand.'

'He did?'

'He did. Mary was like that. Always up to something.'

'What did you do?'

'We had our biggest fight ever. Right there in the church. All over that silly gift. You wouldn't believe the things we said to each other.'

'What happened?'

'While we were arguing John left with Abigail Crump.'

Aunt Octopus laughed.

'You were pretty cross with your sister?'

'Very cross. For that one moment, I actually hated my own sister. Can you imagine that?'

'I can,' said George.

'What happened?'

'Oh, I forgave her later. I could never stay cross with Mary.'

'I suppose there are some things that you can't forgive,' said George. 'Like what I said downstairs.'

Aunt Octavia thought for a moment.

'Do you love Lucky?' she asked.

'Of course.'

'Have you ever been cross with him?'

George remembered one time in a car-park. Lucky would not walk on his lead. He had rolled over and made George pull him. A crowd of people had clapped and cheered for Lucky.

He remembered another time. He had left Lucky in the car for just a moment. When he got back Lucky had torn up the shopping bags and scattered the shopping everywhere.

He remembered one other time. It had been during a baseball game. Lucky had stolen the ball and had started a game of Keep-away on the ball field.

Yes, he had been pretty cross with Lucky.

He nodded at Aunt Octavia. 'Lots of times,' he said.

'Did you forgive him?'

'Of course,' said George. 'I could never

stay cross with Lucky!'

'That's the way I feel about you,' said Aunt Octavia. 'And I'm not cross with Lucky, either. He's just being a dog.'

She wrapped her arms around George and hugged him. He hugged her back and for once he did not think of octopus arms. He smelled her cinnamon smell. Her arms were warm and soft.

'Let's start again,' said Aunt Octavia. 'Let's go downstairs and open the presents and have Christmas.'

She stood up. George didn't get up.

'What's wrong now?' she asked.

'Lucky,' said George. 'Dad wants to send him to the kennel. How can we have Christmas without Lucky?'

'Hmm,' she sat back down. 'I think your father might change his mind about the kennel,' she said. 'But we still need a way to get Lucky out from under the sofa.'

George nodded.

'Maybe he would come out for a dog treat.'

George shook his head.

'A piece of ham?'

George shook his head again. He thought and thought. What would make Lucky come out?

'I have an idea,' Aunt Octavia said. 'I think it's time for me to give Lucky his Christmas present.'

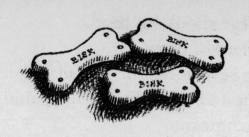

Dog Presents

Lucky waited deep under the sofa. It was quiet now. The people had gone. Even so, he would not come out. He had learned something about hiding from watching the tabby cat next door.

She would wait for hours at a mouse hole. Patiently and quietly she would wait. And then when the mouse finally came out, POUNCE! She always caught it.

Lucky was not taking any chances. Nothing would get him out from under this sofa.

He heard footsteps. He heard the man's voice first.

'Come on, Lucky.'

Lucky sniffed the air.

Sniff sniff.

Dog biscuits.

He would never come out for a dog biscuit.

He waited. More footsteps.

'Come on out, Lucky.'

This time it was the boy's mother.

Sniff sniff.

HAM! His mouth watered.

No. He would not come out. Not even for *HAM*.

He waited. More footsteps.

This time it was the boy and the visitor. He must *not* come out!

Sniff sniff.

He pushed his nose forward and sniffed the air. Could it be?

Sniff sniff.

It must be!

Sniff sniff.

Yes, it was!

The car animal! It was on the floor in front of the sofa!

He dug his nails into the rug. He must not come out.

But he could not resist the smell. He inched forward. Inch by inch. Sniffing and crawling. Sniffing and crawling and . . .

He scrambled out from under the sofa.

POUNCE!

The boy grabbed him. He was caught! The boy hugged him. He put him back down on the floor in front of a paper hump. A big crinkly hump that smelled like the car animal!

Lucky knew about presents. Presents were a game where people hid something in paper and he tore off the paper to find out what it was.

The big present sat in front of him. The irresistible smell told him exactly what it was.

The car animal.

He pounced. He ripped the paper. The pieces of red and green paper came off in long shreds. He ripped and tore the paper

until none was left. He looked at the soft white animal.

It was puffy now like a pillow.

Lucky lunged forward and sank his teeth into it. He shook his head back and forth.

He rolled on it a few times. It was soft and smelled wonderful.

He looked up at the boy and the visitor and the man and the woman.

No one said, 'Bad dog'.

'Merry Christmas, Lucky,' the visitor said.

It was for him!

Dog Heaven.

Recycled!

George watched Lucky roll on the pillow. It was Aunt Octopus's surprise. She had made a pillow for Lucky out of her old sheepskin jacket.

Everything was perfect. The mountain bike gleamed beside the Christmas tree. His mother loved her sign. She had already used it for fifteen hugs. His father liked his dinosaur. He was going to put it on his desk for a paperweight. Aunt Octavia had been so excited about her dance lessons that she did dance steps all around the Christmas tree.

He looked at the tree and all the unwrapped presents. Everything was *almost*

perfect. If only he had a present for Aunt Octavia. The dance lessons were really from his parents. He wished that he had bought her a blue hat like in the story.

It was too late. The shops were closed. Suddenly George had an idea. 'I'll be right back,' he said.

He ran upstairs and in less than a minute returned with a large rectangular panel.

He handed it to Aunt Octavia.

'What can this be?' she asked.

She held it. She felt it. She shook it.

Slowly she pulled off the red wrapping paper.

'Oh,' she said.

George held his breath.

'You shouldn't have.' She dabbed her eyes. 'Elvis, you hound dog!'

Elvis Presley on black velvet.

'Recycled!' said George.

'My favourite kind of gift,' she said. 'It will always remind me of you and my very best Christmas.'

She gave George a big octopus hug.

Joyful Noises

Lucky was lying on his new animal pillow, chewing his new rawhide bone. His back legs pointed straight into the air. The smell of the pillow was all around him. His presents were beside him. His family loved him again.

Dog Heaven!

His people sat around the indoor tree. The boy began to sing. Lucky sat straight up on the pillow and watched. He loved singing.

'Joy to the world, the Lord is come!' The man joined in. Then the boy's mother. Then the visitor.

The visitor! He had never greeted the

visitor. Should he do it now? Why not? Lucky ran to the visitor. She opened her arms and with one jump he was in them. He gave her a big lick. Then another. She liked it. She held him tight.

The singing rang around him.

'Let heaven and nature sing! Let heaven and nature sing!'

It was a happy sound.

Lucky cocked his head once. He knew what to do. He pointed his nose in the air and added his most joyful noise.

AAOOOOO!

Christmas was a good word after all!

A Boy in the Doghouse

Betsy Duffey

**"Cut it out," whispered George.
"It's bedtime! You're supposed to
go to sleep now!"
"ERRRF!"**

George loves his new puppy Lucky, but Lucky
is out of control. If George can't stop Lucky
barking at night and making puddles in the
house, Mum and Dad say he will have to go!

But Lucky is determined to be top dog! He
wants to teach George to give him more ham,
and sleep with him in the doghouse.
So who's training who?

This warm and funny story will
capture the hearts of all young
animal-lovers. It is the first in a
series of books featuring George,
and his lively puppy, Lucky.

THE RAILWAY CAT

Phyllis Arkle

Railway Porter v. Railway Cat. Who will win?

Alfie the railway cat lives at the station where he's a favourite with all the regular passengers. The only trouble is that Hack, the new railway porter, doesn't like cats and he soon has a plan for getting rid of Alfie.

THE RAILWAY CAT AND DIGBY

Phyllis Arkle

Alfie the railway cat is in trouble again!

Somehow Alfie always seems to be in Leading Railman Hack's bad books. He tries very hard to make friends with Hack, but with little success. And when Alfie decides to try and improve matters by 'helping' Hack's dog, Digby, win a prize at the local show, things rapidly go from bad to worse!

FANTASTIC MR FOX

Roald Dahl

Boggis, Bunce and Bean are just about the nastiest and meanest three farmers you could meet.

And they hate Mr Fox. They are determined to get him. So they lie in wait outside his hole, each one crouching behind a tree with his gun loaded, ready to shoot, starve, or dig him out. But clever, handsome Mr Fox has other plans!

THE Hodgeheg

Dick King-Smith

Max is a hedgehog who becomes a hodgeheg, who becomes a hero!

The hedgehog family of Number 5A are a happy bunch, but they dream of reaching the Park. Unfortunately, a very busy road lies between them and their goal and no one has found a way to cross it in safety. No one, that is, until the determined young Max decides to solve the problem once and for all...

Also in Young Puffin

The Swoose

Dick King-Smith

"Are you feather-brained?" said the vole. "No, I'm Fitzherbert."

Fitzherbert is confused. With his oversized feet and snaky neck, he is shunned by the other goslings. Then his mother reveals that he is a rare breed of bird indeed – the offspring of her romantic liaison with a dashing white swan. With stars in his eyes, Fitzherbert sets off in search of his father and discovers fame beyond the farmyard in the household of the Queen of England herself!

'Other writers who put words into animals' mouths are outclassed' – *The Times Educational Supplement*

'Judy Brown's enchanting black and white illustrations capture the spirit of both swoose and sovereign' – *Independent on Sunday*

Also in Young Puffin

A DINOSAUR CALLED MINERVA

Tessa Krailing

From the depths of the cave . . . came a roar so mighty that the ground shook.

Sprog doesn't want to spend his holidays with his nutty great aunt, but when he meets Minerva the adventure of his life begins. Not only is Minerva a dinosaur, but she has a toothache too! Sprog simply has to help, but how can he without anyone knowing about it?

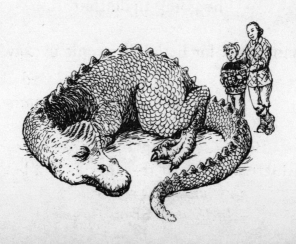

SEPTIMOUSE, SUPERMOUSE!

Ann Jungman

"I, Septimouse, am the seventh son of a seventh son, and have magical powers."

Septimouse is a genius. He can do things that other mice cannot do. He can talk to cats, talk to big people, talk to little big people, and make them as small as mice. But the one thing he really wants to do is to eat some cheese – delicious yellow food that big people use to catch mice – and how on earth is he going to do that?

A funny book for little big people everywhere!

Hairy and Slug

Margaret Joy

Hairy and Slug are quite a team!

TV-mad Hairy, the Mablesdens' large,
brown shaggy dog, and Slug, the family's
incredibly ramshackle little white car,
have the most amazing adventures!
It's surprising how ordinary everyday
outings turn into something quite
different when Hairy and Slug are
around!

SEPTIMOUSE, BIG CHEESE!

Ann Jungman

> **"Big, big people in a trice,
> Be as small as little mice."**

As the seventh son of a seventh son,
Septimouse has amazing magical powers.
When little big person Katie's dad loses his job,
Septimouse has a brilliant plan. He shrinks
big, big person Mum and big, big person Dad,
and takes them through the mouse hole behind
the fridge! There they see the magnificent
mouse cheese factory Septimouse has created.
And from little cheeses big cheeses soon begin
to grow, and Dad gets a new job.

A funny book for
little big people
everywhere!

READ MORE IN PUFFIN

For children of all ages, Puffin represents quality and variety – the very best in publishing today around the world.

For complete information about books available from Puffin – and Penguin – and how to order them, contact us at the appropriate address below. Please note that for copyright reasons the selection of books varies from country to country.

On the worldwide web: www.puffin.co.uk

In the United Kingdom: Please write to *Dept. EP, Penguin Books Ltd, Bath Road, Harmondsworth, West Drayton, Middlesex UB7 0DA*

In the United States: Please write to *Consumer Sales, Penguin USA, P.O. Box 999, Dept. 17109, Bergenfield, New Jersey 07621-0120*. VISA and MasterCard holders call 1-800-253-6476 to order Penguin titles

In Canada: Please write to *Penguin Books Canada Ltd, 10 Alcorn Avenue, Suite 300, Toronto, Ontario M4V 3B2*

In Australia: Please write to *Penguin Books Australia Ltd, P.O. Box 257, Ringwood, Victoria 3134*

In New Zealand: Please write to *Penguin Books (NZ) Ltd, Private Bag 102902, North Shore Mail Centre, Auckland 10*

In India: Please write to *Penguin Books India Pvt Ltd, 706 Eros Apartments, 56 Nehru Place, New Delhi 110 019*

In the Netherlands: Please write to *Penguin Books Netherlands bv, Postbus 3507, NL-1001 AH Amsterdam*

In Germany: Please write to *Penguin Books Deutschland GmbH, Metzlerstrasse 26, 60594 Frankfurt am Main*

In Spain: Please write to *Penguin Books S. A., Bravo Murillo 19, 1° B, 28015 Madrid*

In Italy: Please write to *Penguin Italia s.r.l., Via Felice Casati 20, I–20124 Milano*

In France: Please write to *Penguin France S. A., 17 rue Lejeune, F–31000 Toulouse*

In Japan: Please write to *Penguin Books Japan, Ishikiribashi Building, 2–5–4, Suido, Bunkyo-ku, Tokyo 112*

In South Africa: Please write to *Longman Penguin Southern Africa (Pty) Ltd, Private Bag X08, Bertsham 2013*